How to Catch

STORYBOOK COLLECTION

From the *New York Times* bestselling team
Adam Wallace & Andy Elkerton

sourcebooks
wonderland

Contents

How to Catch a Mermaid 1

How to Catch a Snowman 33

How to Catch a Leprechaun 65

How to Catch a Unicorn.. 95

How to Catch a Dragon...127

How to Catch a Dinosaur 159

How to Catch a Monster 191

How to Catch a Yeti...223

253

Copyright © 2021 by Sourcebooks
Text by Adam Wallace
Illustrations by Andy Elkerton
Cover and internal design © 2021 by Sourcebooks

The art was first sketched, then painted digitally with brushes designed by the artist.

Published by Sourcebooks Wonderland, an imprint of Sourcebooks Kids
Sourcebooks, 1935 Brookdale Rd., Naperville, IL, 60563
(630) 961-3900
sourcebookskids.com

The Library of Congress Cataloging-in-Publication data is on file with the publisher.

Source of Production: Hung Hing Off-Set Printing Co. Ltd., Shenzhen, Guangdong Province, China
Date of Production: June 2021
Run Number: 5022029

Printed and bound in China.
HH 10 9 8 7 6 5 4 3 2 1